Claudia Martin

Oceans at Work

Illustrated by
Fiona Osbaldstone

WAYLAND
www.waylandbooks.co.uk

First published in 2021 in Great Britain by Wayland
Copyright © Hodder and Stoughton 2021

Produced for Wayland by
White-Thomson Publishing Ltd
www.wtpub.co.uk

ISBN: 978 1 5263 1435 2 (HB) 978 1 5263 1436 9 (PB)

Credits
Author and editor: Claudia Martin
Illustrator: Fiona Osbaldstone
Designer: Dan Prescott, Couper Street Type Co.
Proofreader: Annabel Savery

The publisher would like to thank the following for permission to reproduce their photographs:
Alamy: Matthieu Paley/National Geographic Image Collection 4r, Christian Goupi/Agefotostock 15, Yay Media AS 19, WaterFrame_tfr 27, Robert Harding 28; Getty Images: Tony Beck/500px 4l, Monty Rakusen 7, ssuaphoto/istock 24; Shutterstock: Lukasz Z 5tl, RaksyBH 5tr, Karin Riethoven 5b, Val Shevchenko 9, Ana Flasker 10, Oscar Espinosa 13, soft_light 16, tcly 20, noomcpk 23.

Every attempt has been made to clear copyright. Should there be any
inadvertent omission please apply to the publisher for rectification.

The website addresses (URLs) included in this book were valid at the time of going to press.
However, it is possible that contents or addresses may have changed since the publication of this
book. No responsibility for any such changes can be accepted by either the author or the Publisher.

Printed in Dubai

Wayland, an imprint of
Hachette Children's Group
Part of Hodder and Stoughton
Carmelite House
50 Victoria Embankment
London EC4Y 0DZ

An Hachette UK Company
www.hachette.co.uk
www.hachettechildrens.co.uk

Contents

Oceans at Work

Across the world, millions of people are at work in and around the five oceans. Through their hard work, the oceans give us food, resources, transport, energy and fun. Yet when we make use of the oceans, we must remember to protect their water, animals and plants for the future.

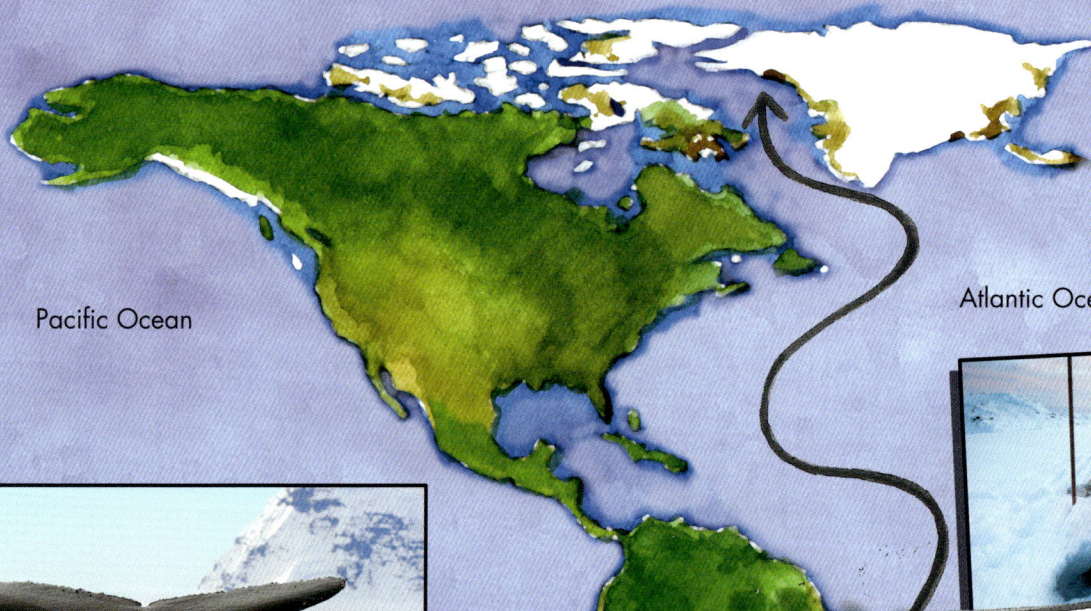

Pacific Ocean

Atlantic Ocean

Southern Ocean

Fun

Holiday-makers have fun on beaches or sailing across the ocean to see whales and distant islands.

Food

People use nets, traps and hooks to catch fish and other sea creatures to eat.

Farming Seaweed

Seaweed is a plant-like living thing that is found in the ocean.

People use seaweed in cooking, medicine, farms and factories.

Some seaweed is good to eat. In Japan, in the Pacific Ocean, nori seaweed is dried and pressed into sheets, then wrapped around rice. In Wales, laver seaweed is cooked into a tasty paste called laverbread. Seaweed can also be made into food for farm animals, dressings for wounds, and products from toothpaste to paint.

Seaweed may float through the ocean, or cling to rocks or the seabed. Some people know how to collect wild seaweed along the shore. Others build seaweed farms in shallow water. They drive poles into the sand, then string lines or nets between them. They release seaweed seeds, called spores. The spores attach to the lines and begin to grow.

Collecting Salt

The ocean tastes salty because of the countless salty particles that float in it.

Humans use sea salt in food, soap, plastic and pottery.

The oceans began to grow salty as soon as they formed, around 4 billion years ago. When rainwater and rivers rush over rocks, they wear away specks of salty minerals. These specks are carried to the ocean. Sea salt is collected from shallow seawater in salt farms. When the water is heated by the Sun, it evaporates, turning to gas and drifting away. The solid salt is left behind.

Humans must not drink seawater, because our bodies cannot cope with too much salt. In hot countries where there is not enough rain to fill rivers and lakes, giant seaside factories can turn seawater into drinking water by removing the salt.

Pearl Diving

For thousands of years, bright pearls have been placed in crowns, rings and necklaces.

Pearls are made in the shells of sea creatures such as pearl oysters.

Pearl oysters live inside a hinged shell, often along the coasts of the Indian and Pacific Oceans. If a grain of sand or a tiny creature enters the oyster's shell, the oyster makes smooth, hard nacre to wrap around the intruder. When nacre catches the light, it shines in all the colours of the rainbow. Eventually, a beautiful pearl is formed.

In the past, brave divers risked their lives to find pearls, holding their breath as they swam to the seabed. In Japan, the female, white-robed Ama pearlers still dive without using air tanks. Most pearls on sale today are from farms, where the oysters live in hanging baskets that can be lifted from the water.

Seaside Holidays

Everyone loves to splash in the foaming waves or build towering sandcastles.

Across the world, people head to the beach for day trips and happy holidays.

Some beach-goers stay on dry land, reading books under a palm tree or looking for crabs in rock pools. Others test their skills by taking lessons in surfing or sailing. Some breathe air through short tubes called snorkels as they swim, watching colourful fish in the water.

When people take seaside holidays, they bring money to the coast. Local people find work in hotels, restaurants and entertainment. Yet holiday-making can also damage the coast and ocean, if careless crowds and vast hotels make litter, mess and noise. Care must be taken of the spots where seabirds lay their eggs and sea turtles dig their precious nests in the sand.

Fun at Sea

**In search of adventure, people
set sail across the oceans.**

**They hoist sails on yachts or
buy tickets for colossal cruise ships.**

A cruise ship is a floating hotel, housing as many as 8,000 holiday-makers and staff. Passengers can step ashore at elegant coastal cities, such as Italy's Venice or Australia's Sydney. Some ocean adventurers take shorter trips, spending an afternoon watching for whales or gazing at coral reefs in a glass-bottomed boat. Skilled sailors steer their yachts through Caribbean Islands or race them across the Atlantic Ocean.

All ocean-going ships must be sure not to leak waste or oil from their engines. The larger the ship, the louder the buzz of its engines, which can worry whales and dolphins. Captains should not sail near delicate habitats, such as coral reefs and beds of seagrass.

Carrying Cargo

Every day, thousands of cargo ships make their way across the oceans.

Cargo ships carry vast amounts of products from one port to another.

Bulk ships carry coal, metal or grain, such as wheat or barley. They have huge below-deck areas, called holds, for storing them. Tanker ships have tanks for carrying oil. Cars, machines and furniture are carried by container ship. The products are loaded into truck-sized metal containers, which are stacked on the deck.

The largest container ships are 400m long. For days or weeks, the ships sail hundreds or thousands of kilometres. When ships reach port, the containers are unloaded by towering cranes then continue their journey by train or lorry. Around 25 million containers are loaded and unloaded every year in the busy port of Singapore, in the Indian Ocean.

Oil and Gas

Oil and natural gas are useful fuels that can be found beneath the ocean floor.

To reach the fuels, workers build strong structures in the ocean, called rigs.

Oil is used as a fuel in car engines and as an ingredient in plastic. Natural gas is often burned to heat houses or for cooking. Oil and gas formed over millions of years as dead animals and plants were covered and pressed by mud.

On an oil rig, brave workers drill into the seabed, then pump up the fuel. This is difficult and dangerous work. The fuel is taken to land by tanker or a pipe on the seabed. Workers are very careful, but if there is an accident, oil can leak out and coat the fur or feathers of sea creatures. This means they struggle to float and stay warm. Another problem with these fuels is that they release a gas called carbon dioxide when burned. This gas traps the Sun's heat. If there is too much of it, it makes our planet warmer, a problem that is often called 'global warming' (see page 26).

Making Electricity

Ocean water is always moving, as the wind whips up waves and tides rise then fall.

This movement can be turned into electricity, without making pollution.

Tides are caused by gravity, a force that pulls objects towards each other. As the Moon pulls on Earth, the sea bulges towards it. As Earth turns, the moving bulge makes tides, with the sea rising up the shore then drawing back. Special machines use the rushing water of waves and tides to turn wheels, called turbines. Turbines power generators, which make electricity.

Turbines on tall poles are turned by the wind to make electricity. Wind turbines are often placed in coastal waters, where the wind is strong and they do not spoil the view. The electricity is taken to land by underwater cables.

Studying the Sea

Scientists study ocean animals so they can keep them safe.

They can travel deep into the oceans in underwater ships called submersibles.

When an animal is at risk of extinction, scientists may capture some adults so they can have babies in a safe place. When the babies are big enough, they can be released back into the ocean. Scientists also study how global warming is making the ocean hotter, which makes it expand and rise. They warn that, one day, the rising ocean could flood coastal cities. Scientists watch how ice is melting in the Arctic and Southern Oceans, which endangers the animals, such as polar bears, that live on the ice.

Scientists use submersibles to study underwater volcanoes and ground movements that could set off a giant wave, called a tsunami. If scientists think a tsunami could happen, they warn everyone who lives near the coast.

Shipbuilding

**Ships must be strong, long-lasting
and able to float.**

**Some shipbuilders carve wood,
while others melt and hammer metal.**

Materials that float are less dense than water, which means their tiny particles are less tightly packed. These materials feel light. Long ago, people noticed that wood floats on water. Today, some shipbuilders still make traditional boats from wood. In the Pacific Islands, outrigger canoes are made of a hollowed tree trunk, with a wooden outrigger, or float, for balance.

Racing canoes and yachts (see pages 18–19) are made from super-light materials, such as fibreglass. They are smoothly shaped, so they slip quickly through the water. Cargo ships (see page 21) are built from strong, heavy materials, such as steel. They float because they are filled with air rather than being solid, in the same way a balloon floats into the sky.

Captions for Photographs

On the chilly Atlantic Ocean, a fisherman empties a net full of fish into his trawler.

Sri Lankan fishermen perch on poles in the shallows, waiting for fish to nibble at the bait on their lines.

On the coast of Indonesia, in Southeast Asia, seaweed is harvested from a beach-side farm.

Salt is raked into piles ready for collection in a salt farm in Vietnam, on the shores of the Indian Ocean.

Off the coast of the Japanese city of Toba, an Ama pearl diver takes the plunge.

A snorkeller captures photos of life on a coral reef, in warm, sunlit Philippine waters.

Traditional wooden boats called pirogues take part in a race off the coast of Mauritius, in the Indian Ocean.

Containers of goods are unloaded in the port of Qingdao, on China's Pacific Ocean coast.

A crane lifts workers off an oil rig in the Gulf of Thailand, a sea of the western Pacific Ocean.

In the North Sea, wind turbines make electricity for homes, factories, offices and schools.

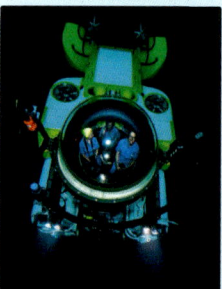

Scientists journey deep beneath the water surface in the *DeepSee* submersible, near the Pacific Ocean's Cocos Island.

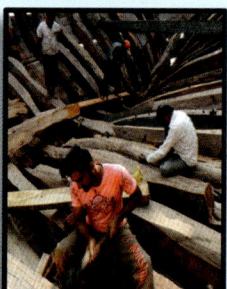

Carpenters build a large wooden boat called a dhow, in the Indian port of Mandvi.

Glossary

bait food placed on a hook to attract fish

carbon dioxide a gas that is found naturally in the air and is also released by burning the fuels oil, gas and coal

cargo materials and products that are carried by ship or other transportation

coastal near the coast, where the ocean meets the land

coral reef a stony underwater ridge made of the skeletons of millions of tiny animals called coral polyps

dense tightly packed

energy power that can be used to drive machines or to create heat and light

expand to grow bigger

extinction when the last living member of a group of animals dies

fibreglass a machine-made material containing plastic and threads of glass

fuel a material burned to make heat

gas a substance, such as air, that is neither liquid nor solid

generator a machine that converts movement into electricity

global warming the rising of the temperatures of Earth's air and oceans, caused largely by human activities

habitat the natural home of a group of animals and plants

mineral a solid material that is found naturally in Earth's rocks or ocean

nacre a smooth, hard material made by some sea animals

natural gas a mixture of gases that is found inside Earth's rocks and can be burned as a fuel

oil a liquid fuel found inside Earth's rocks

particle a tiny portion of matter

pollution releasing harmful materials or energy into the ocean, air, or soil

port a town or city where ships load and unload

product something made or grown that can be sold

resource a material that can be useful

species a group of animals that look similar to each other and can make babies together

spore a cell, released by seaweeds and some other living things, that can grow into a new living thing

submersible a small boat that can travel underwater

turbine a machine with blades, or arms, that are turned by the movement or water or air

yacht a boat with sails or an engine that is used for pleasure or racing

Further Reading

Books

Deep-Sea Fishing (Dangerous Jobs), Erin Palmer (Escape, 2019)

Research on the Edge, Angela Royston (Wayland, 2014)

Seas and Oceans (Fact Cat: Geography), Izzi Howell (Wayland, 2016)

The Oil Industry (Development or Destruction), Richard Spilsbury (Wayland, 2014)

Websites

Find out more about ocean jobs on these websites:

https://kids.kiddle.co/Fishing_industry

https://science.howstuffworks.com/environmental/energy/oil-drilling-process.htm

https://www.amnh.org/explore/ology/marine-biology

https://www.nhm.ac.uk/discover/oceans.html

Index

THE OCEANS EXPLORED

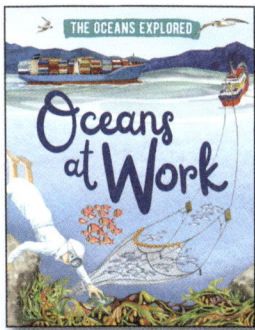

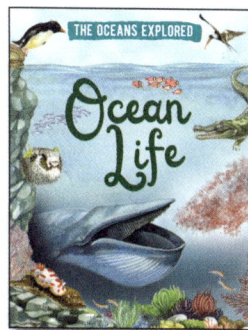

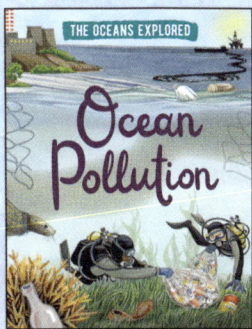

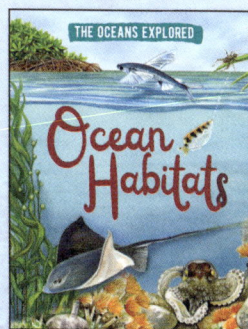